To: Theo

Rhyme, Rhyme All The Time

I hope you enjoy my rhymes!

www.nubianamedia.com

S Rodgers

x

Rhyme, Rhyme All The Time

There is something magical,
About poetry that rhymes.
You can predict the words,
Most of the time.

-Samantha Rodgers

Contents

The Library

We're going to the library.
We're going to have a look,
At all of the wonderful,
Different types of books.

There are books with pictures.
Stories filled with rhymes.
Books packed with excitement,
To read all the time.

We get to choose two books,
That we can take home,
To read with our parents,
Or to read alone.

The library is filled with story gems.
It's like a treasure chest.
Of all the places in my school,
The library is the best!

Paint!

Paint! Paint!
It's all over the chair.
Paint! Paint!
It's even in my hair.
Paint! Paint!
It's all over the floor.
Paint! Paint!
It's even on the door.

Paint! Paint!
It's all over the place.
Paint! Paint!
It's even on my face.
Paint! Paint!
Please take care.
Paint! Paint!
It's going everywhere!

Glitter

Whenever I've used glitter,
I notice that people stare.
Then they stop to tell me,
That there's glitter in my hair.

It's not easy to get rid of,
And no matter how hard you try,
It seems as if glitter,
Simply falls down from the sky.

Glitter is bright and sparkly,
I sprinkle it without care.
That's why most of the glitter,
Ends up everywhere.

Even after I shower,
It always reappears.
I always find some glitter,
Stuck behind my ears.

Playtime

Our favourite time at school,
Is when we go out to play.
We like being with our friends,
And playing with them every day.

We go up and down the slide,
And the climbing frame.
We enjoy our time outside,
Playing lots of games.

I love going on the swings,
Swinging really high.
I often sit and wonder,
If I'll ever reach the sky.

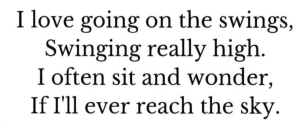

Hide and Seek

I love playing hide and seek.
I like to hide and see,
If my friends will take forever,
Looking everywhere for me.

I can hide under the table.
I can hide behind the chairs.
I can hide in the sandpit.
They'll never find me there.

But if I could be invisible,
It would be interesting to see,
My friend's confused faces,
When they try to find me!

My Skipping Rope

I love my new skipping rope.
It's really very cool.
My dad said that I am allowed,
To take it into school.
I practise every day at break,
Jumping with my feet.
I chant a rhyme each time I skip,
And never miss a beat.
While I am skipping,
I can even run and hop.
I'm getting so much better.
Now, I never want to stop.

The Maze

I'm stuck inside the maze.
 Which way should I go?
Turn left or turn right?
 I really don't know.

 I need to find the exit.
 I've been running up and down.
 Back and forth, back and forth,
 Running all around.

The maze is fantastic.
 We're having bags of fun.
I can see the exit.
 Hooray! I've won!

Building Blocks

I like playing with building blocks.
I pile them high on top.
I like to see how far I'll reach,
Until they fall and drop.
I never give up,
And keep adding some more.
Oh no! They're going to topple.
They've all dropped to the floor!

Tidy Up

When it's time to tidy up,
We work well as a team.
Helping one another,
To keep things nice and clean.

We tidy up quickly.
It never takes too long,
To put our toys back,
In the box where they belong.

Lunch Box

In my school lunch box.
Are amazing treats.
Mouthwatering snacks,
To enjoy and eat.

A crisp juicy apple.
A delicious cupcake.
That melts in your mouth,
With every bite you take.

A nice slice of pizza,
With melted cheese on top.
Freshly squeezed orange juice.
No fizzy pop!

A strawberry yoghurt.
A healthy cereal bar.
Some seedless grapes,
In a small plastic jar.

When I open my lunch box,
Food is always on my mind.
I'm always curious,
To see what I will find.

I'm never disappointed.
I love everything I see.
My snacks are very tasty,
Made especially for me.

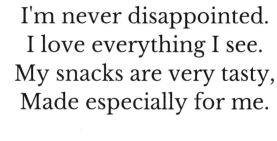

Birthday Party

I'm going to a party.
I don't want to be late.
I am so excited.
I know it will be great.
There will be lovely balloons,
And sparkling decorations.
Party hats and streamers.
An amazing celebration.

There'll be lovely party foods.
An impressive birthday cake.
I'll also get a goody bag,
That I'm allowed to take.
I'm sure that it will be,
Filled with delicious treats.
I'm really looking forward,
To some tasty yummy sweets.

There will be party games.
So much fun to share.
Playing pass the parcel,
And even musical chairs.
I love going to parties,
They are simply divine.
Soon it will be my birthday,
Then the party will be mine!

Jelly

I love jelly.
It always wobble, wobbles.
I love the way it tastes
So I always gobble, gobble.

I love making jelly,
Pouring it into the mould,
To set in the fridge,
Until it's nice and cold.

Jelly with ice cream
Is a great combination.
I wish that I could live,
In a wobbly jelly nation.

Ice Cream

Ice cream is so scrumptious.
I love the way it tastes.
Whenever I have ice cream,
It never goes to waste.

When the ice cream starts to melt,
It drips and it lingers.
Then I make a mess,
And end up with sticky fingers.

I usually ask for two scoops,
Heaped high on the cone.
I never have any problems,
Eating ice cream on my own.

Movie Time

We love watching movies.
It's such a fabulous treat.
Movies packed with excitement,
Make us jump out of our seats.

We enjoy eating popcorn,
Hot dogs and ice cream.
Potato chips and cookies,
Makes movie time supreme.

Popcorn

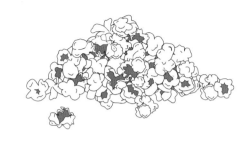

Pop, pop, popcorn.
Salty or sweet.
Pop, pop, popcorn,
A delicious tasty treat.
Pop, pop, popcorn.
With cheese or caramel.
Pop, pop, popcorn.
I love the way it smells.
Pop, pop, popcorn.
I wish it was okay,
To eat crunchy popcorn,
Every single day.

Cupcakes

I have all the ingredients,
That I need to make,
A deliciously tasty,
Batch of cupcakes.

I'll cream the sugar and butter,
Then mix in the flour.
Add milk and some eggs,
In less than one hour.

I'll pop the cakes in the oven,
Making sure they're safely in.
Then I'll tidy up the kitchen,
And let the baking begin.

The smell is amazing,
And right before my eyes.
I'm watching the mixture,
Slowly starting to rise.

The cupcakes are ready.
They are fluffy and light.
I've added some creamy topping.
What a beautiful sight!

My stomach is rumbling.
There's no time to waste.
It's time to tuck in,
To see how they taste.

Feelings

Sometimes, I feel happy.
Sometimes, I feel sad.
Sometimes, I feel lonely.
Sometimes, I feel bad.

Sometimes, I feel anxious.
Sometimes, I feel excited.
Sometimes, I feel scared.
Sometimes, I feel delighted.

Sometimes, I feel nervous.
Sometimes, I feel cheerful.
Sometimes, I feel angry.
Sometimes, I feel tearful.

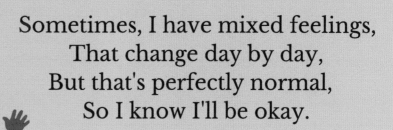

Sometimes, I have mixed feelings,
That change day by day,
But that's perfectly normal,
So I know I'll be okay.

Share

It's always good to share,
And show that you care.
When you fuss and fight,
It's not a pretty sight.
When you are kind,
You will always find,
That people will do,
Nice things for you too.

Sorry

Today, I upset my friend.
At first, I didn't know why,
He was so upset,
Until I saw him cry.

I never meant to hurt him,
When I took his teddy bear.
We always play together.
And we always share.

I hope that he's okay.
I don't want him to worry.
I'll make sure that I ask next time.
Then told him I was sorry.

Say Please!

When the wind blows,
We feel a slight breeze.
When water turns to ice,
   It needs to freeze.

     When we're at school,
      We learn our ABCs.
     When we have our photo taken,
      We're asked to say, 'Cheese!'

When we have a tickly nose.
We often loudly sneeze.
When we jump and land,
We always bend our knees.

     So whenever we ask for something,
      It should be with ease,
      To remember our manners,
      And politely say, 'PLEASE!'

Say PLEASE!

The Mirror

When I look in the mirror,
What do I see?
A reflection that looks,
Just like me!
We have the same face.
We have the same eyes.
We have the same smile.
An identical surprise.
We have the same hair.
We have the same ears.
When I look in the mirror,
My twin always appears.
I love my reflection,
And all that I see.
I am unique.
There's only one me!

My Mummy's Tummy

My mummy is having a baby.
I'm watching her tummy grow.
I'm not sure if it's a boy or girl,
But I really want to know.

I'm getting really excited,
But at times I start to fear,
That my mummy will forget me,
When the new baby is here.

My mummy gave me a cuddle,
And told me not to feel so blue,
She said she'll love the baby,
And will always love me too!

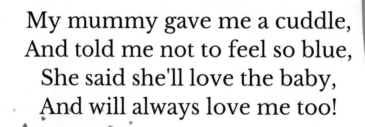

My Baby Sister

My baby sister is so cute.
She loves to suck her dummy.
Then when she needs her nappy changed,
She cries out for our mummy.

She gets herself into a mess,
Like when her nose is runny.
It trickles down on to her lips,
It always looks so funny.

She tries to wipe it all away,
But the tissue sticks to her nose,
And then the tissue follows her,
Wherever my sister goes.

Sometimes she has a tantrum,
When she gets into a muddle,
But I'm always there to help.
Then I give her a big cuddle.

Twins

Being a twin is great.
We care about each other.
We are a dynamic duo.
The best sister and brother.
We look very similar.
We share the same genes.
In our loving family,
We're an unbeatable team.
We are individuals,
But it is clear to see,
We come as a package.
Buy one, get one free!

Our Grandparents

Our grandparents are special,
We love it when they're in town.
It's always so much fun,
Having them around.

They like sharing stories,
About memories from their past.
We cling on to their every word.
It's always such a blast.

They always make us laugh,
And give great cuddles too.
We're so happy when they visit.
We love everything they do.

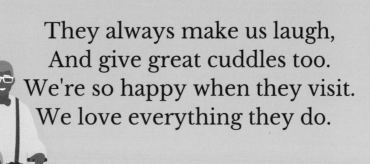

Holiday

We're going on holiday.
We're going on a plane.
I'm so excited,
To travel once again.

I've got my suitcase ready.
There are so many things to bring.
I'm hoping that I won't forget,
To pack important things.

My teddy bear is coming,
So he won't be left alone.
I was worried that he'd be sad,
Being at home on his own.

We've got our passports ready.
We're all checked in.
I'm really excited,
For our adventure to begin.

We're on board the plane.
Up, up and away,
High into the skies,
To start our holiday.

The Beach

When I go to the beach,
I love paddling in the sea.
Splashing in the water,
Always makes me feel happy.

The beach is wonderful,
With dazzling sparkling sand.
I love the way the sand feels.
When I hold it in my hands.

I always take my bucket,
And my lovely spade,
So I can show my daddy,
All the sandcastles I've made.

I enjoy collecting shells.
There are lovely ones to see.
When I'm at the beach,
I'm as happy as can be.

40

Scuba Duba

If I could make,
One fabulous wish.
I'd live underwater,
In the sea with the fish.

I could see all of the animals,
That live deep within the sea.
They'd become my best friends,
And could always play with me.

I would be so happy,
Swimming freely up and down.
My new home would be in the water.
The best address in town.

The Weather

The weather always changes.
Sometimes, it's too hot.
Sometimes, it's too cold,
And some days it's not.

Sometimes, it's cloudy,
And the sky looks grey.
That's always a clear sign,
That the rain is on its way.

Sometimes, it's windy,
So it's good to know,
Just how strong,
The gales of wind will blow.

The weather always changes.
It never needs a reason.
To go from hot to cold,
Because of the four seasons.

Rainbow Ride

If I could ride on a rainbow,
I would cheer out loud.
Whizzing through the sky.
Sitting on fluffy clouds.

I would touch the bright colours,
As they illuminate the sky,
Then wave to the birds,
As they quickly glide by.

I would slide down the rainbow,
And have so much fun,
Then when the sky is clear,
I would smile and meet the sun.

43

My Strange Pets

I had a dog,
That turned into a frog.
I had a cat,
That turned into a bat.

I had no idea,
Why my pets had changed.
It was really weird,
And definitely strange.

So my parents said,
'No more pets!'
Until I can turn,
Into a vet.

Busy Bee

I'm a busy, busy bee,
As happy as can be.
Flying all around,
For everyone to see.

I'm a busy, busy bee,
As happy as can be.
Making lots of honey
And then I quickly flee.

I'm a busy, busy bee,
As happy as can be.
Buzz, buzz, buzz.
You can't catch me!

Seat Belt

When I'm going on a journey,
With my parents in the car.
My seat belt is always fastened,
Whether we travel near or far.

It doesn't matter who I'm with.
I never make a fuss.
I also wear my seat belt,
When I'm on the school bus.

It helps to keep me safe,
So I never ever dare,
To forget to wear my seatbelt,
When I travel anywhere.

From Trike to Bike

I have a brand new trike.
I love the way it feels,
When I'm riding in the park,
With its shiny wheels.

But when I get older,
I hope my dream comes true.
My bike won't need three wheels,
Instead, it will have two.

I'll learn how to balance,
And try not to fall.
This will be the greatest,
Challenge of them all.

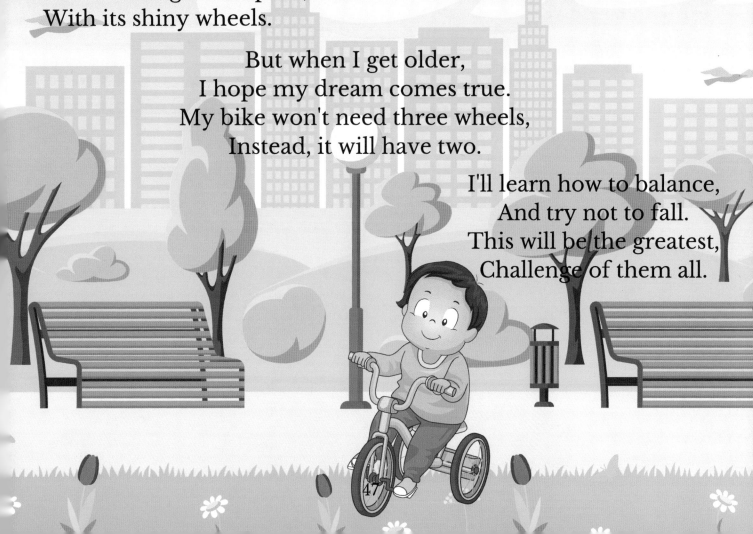

47

Space Trip

If I could go in a rocket,
And fly to outer space.
I wonder what I would see,
In this galactic place?
Will I encounter aliens,
With more than one head?
Or stumble upon new planets,
Where other species live instead?
Will it be scary,
Being up there all alone?
I think I'll be okay,
As long as I can get back home.

Superhero

I want to be a superhero.
One that can fly.
With supersonic speed,
Whizzing through the sky.
My evil opponents,
Will find it difficult to escape.
I'll chase them in my costume,
With my purple bulletproof cape.
I'll use my superpowers,
To help others all the time.
I'll be the bravest superhero,
Preventing treacherous crimes.
I'll stand up against evil,
Leaving villains in a whirl.
Making the world much safer.
For every boy and girl.

Dancing

I'm always very active,
So whenever there's a chance,
For me to get moving,
I jump up and dance.

I love the rhythm of music,
The sounds and the beat.
It makes me so excited.
I can't control my feet.

I like to keep dancing,
To the sounds of the groove.
Swinging my hips,
Every time I move.

I love to express myself,
And release my energy.
Dancing is so wonderful,
For you and for me.

Stretch

It's good to warm up,
Whenever you begin,
To start any exercise,
It helps to stretch your limbs.

Take long deep breaths,
Then gradually exhale.
Stretch your body as slowly,
As a slimy snail.

Stretch your arms out wide.
Touch the tips of your toes.
Then relax your body.
Unwind and simply flow.

Bubbles

Bathtime is wonderful,
With bubbles everywhere.
When I'm soaking in the tub,
I don't have any cares.
My rubber duck is with me.
It keeps me company.
I love the way the water feels.
It's soft and so bubbly.
Whenever it is bathtime,
I always enjoy,
Blowing all the bubbles.
I'm filled with smiles and joy.

My Teeth

I always brush my teeth,
Up and down and deep beneath.
I love the tingly taste,
Of my minty toothpaste.
I brush thoroughly in between,
To make sure they are clean.
Brushing far at the back,
To get rid of all the plaque.
I put my toothbrush down.
Gargle mouthwash all around.
Brushing daily is worthwhile.
To maintain a sparkling smile.
My teeth are nice and bright.
They are such a dazzling sight.

My Tablet

Last night in bed,
I cried and cried,
Because my tablet's battery died.

The screen went blank.
I heard a bleep,
As if it said, 'It's time to sleep!'

I was upset.
I was feeling sad.
I screamed out loudly for my dad.

He came into my bedroom,
And said, 'It's a sign.'
'No more games! It's your bedtime.'

Dreams

When I got to bed,
I eagerly close my eyes.
I always look forward,
To a wonderful surprise.

I'm never really sure,
What my dreams really mean.
I'm never really sure,
About the images, I've seen.

My dreams are very special,
But at times I really hate,
When I wake up in the middle,
Of a dream that's really great.

I love to fall asleep,
Watching the movies in my mind.
Excited about new adventures,
My dreams always find.

Wake Up

When it's time to wake up,
I try to pretend,
That I'm still sleeping,
So my snooze won't have to end.

I love being snuggled,
With the covers over my head.
I wish I could stay forever,
Tucked up warmly in my bed.

Printed in Great Britain
by Amazon

87139457R00033